MADISON S.T.E.A.M.
ACADEMY

Put Beginning Readers on the Right Track with
ALL ABOARD READING™

The All Aboard Reading series is especially designed for beginning readers. Written by noted authors and illustrated in full color, these are books that children really want to read—books to excite their imagination, expand their interests, make them laugh, and support their feelings. With fiction and nonfiction stories that are high interest and curriculum-related, All Aboard Reading books offer something for every young reader. And with four different reading levels, the All Aboard Reading series lets you choose which books are most appropriate for your children and their growing abilities.

Picture Readers
Picture Readers have super-simple texts, with many nouns appearing as rebus pictures. At the end of each book are 24 flash cards—on one side is a rebus picture; on the other side is the written-out word.

Station Stop 1
Station Stop 1 books are best for children who have just begun to read. Simple words and big type make these early reading experiences more comfortable. Picture clues help children to figure out the words on the page. Lots of repetition throughout the text helps children to predict the next word or phrase—an essential step in developing word recognition.

Station Stop 2
Station Stop 2 books are written specifically for children who are reading with help. Short sentences make it easier for early readers to understand what they are reading. Simple plots and simple dialogue help children with reading comprehension.

Station Stop 3
Station Stop 3 books are perfect for children who are reading alone. With longer text and harder words, these books appeal to children who have mastered basic reading skills. More complex stories captivate children who are ready for more challenging books.

In addition to All Aboard Reading books, look for All Aboard Math Readers™ (fiction stories that teach math concepts children are learning in school) and All Aboard Science Readers™ (nonfiction books that explore the most fascinating science topics in age-appropriate language).

All Aboard for happy reading!

For the real Dan, Kate, Ann,
Pete, and Mike, with love—M.E.B.

For Mom and Pops with love—S.S.

Text copyright © 2002 by Grosset & Dunlap. Illustrations copyright © 2002 by Sami Sweeten.
All rights reserved. Published by Grosset & Dunlap, a division of Penguin Putnam Books for
Young Readers, 345 Hudson Street, New York, NY, 10014. ALL ABOARD MATH READER
and GROSSET & DUNLAP are trademarks of Penguin Putnam Inc. Published simultaneously
in Canada. Printed in the U.S.A.

Library of Congress Cataloging-in-Publication Data

Bryant, Megan E.
    Shape spotters / by Megan E. Bryant ; illustrated by Sami Sweeten.
    p. cm.
    "All aboard math reader, station stop 1."
    Summary: The students in Ms. Carey's class look all around the school to find different
shapes.
    [1. Shape—Fiction. 2. Schools—Fiction.] I. Sweeten, Sami, ill. II. Title.
PZ7.B8398 Sh 2002
[E]—dc21
                                                  2002004655

ISBN 0-448-42858-X (pbk)   A B C D E F G H I J

ISBN 0-448-42873-3 (GB)   A B C D E F G H I J

SHAPE SPOTTERS

By Megan E. Bryant
Illustrated by Sami Sweeten

Grosset & Dunlap • New York

Ms. Carey's class is hunting
for shapes.

They hunt for a shape
in the library.

The shape has four sides.
It is not a square.
Look around you.
It's everywhere!

Dan sees some books.

The books are rectangles.

A rectangle has four sides.

It is not square.

All the kids pick up rectangles.

They hunt for a shape
in the music room.

The shape has three sides.
Hear it ring.
It is not a bell.
But it goes
ping, ping, ping.

Kate sees a triangle.

It has three sides.

It goes ping, ping, ping.

All the kids get triangles.
All the kids go
ping, ping, ping.

13

They hunt for a shape
outside.

The shape has no beginning.

The shape has no end.

It goes around and around.

It curves and it bends.

Ann sees some hoops.

The hoops are circles.

A circle has no beginning.

It has no end.

It goes around and around.

All the kids play with circles.

They hunt for a shape
in the lunch room.

The shape has four sides,
all exactly the same.

It's not a rectangle.

Do you know its name?

Pete sees some
sandwiches.

The sandwiches
are squares.

20

A square has
four sides.

All four sides
are the same.

21

Ms. Carey says,
"Watch this."

22

Look! Two rectangles.

Look! Two triangles.

All the kids eat
squares, rectangles,
and triangles for lunch.

Hay School Media Center

They hunt for a shape
in the art room.

The shape is not a square.

The shape is not a rectangle.

It has four sides.

It is turned on an angle.

Mike sees some cutouts.

The cutouts are diamonds.

A diamond has four sides.

It is not a square

or a rectangle.

28

All the kids make pictures
with the diamonds.

The bell rings.

It is time to go home.

Wait! There is one more shape!

It is a star.

All the kids get stars.

Ms. Carey says,
"Great work, shape spotters!
See you tomorrow."

Did you find all the shapes?
There are more.
Go back and look
for the hidden shapes
in the pictures!